DAVY
AND SNAKE

Friends?

AMANDA McCARDIE

ILLUSTRATED BY SUE HEAP

RED FOX

For Oliver

A Red Fox Book

Published by Random House Children's Books
20 Vauxhall Bridge Road, London, SW1V 2SA

A division of The Random House Group Ltd
London Melbourne Sydney Auckland
Johannesburg and agencies throughout the world

Copyright © text Amanda McCardie 2000
Copyright © illustrations Sue Heap 2000

1 3 5 7 9 10 8 6 4 2
First Published by Red Fox 2000

This book is sold subject to the condition that it shall not, by way
of trade or otherwise, be lent, resold, hired out, or otherwise circulated
without the publisher's prior consent in any form of binding or cover
other than that in which it is published and without a similar condition
including this condition being imposed on the subsequent purchaser.

The right of Amanda McCardie to be identified as the author of this work has been
asserted by her in accordance with the Copyright, Designs and Patents Act, 1988.

Printed and bound in Denmark by Nørhaven A/S

Papers used by Random House are natural, recyclable products made from wood
grown in sustainable forests. The manufacturing processes conform to the environ-
mental regulations of the country of origin.

The Random House Group Limited Reg. No. 954009
www.randomhouse.co.uk

ISBN 0 09 940 1797

1

How Davy Found Snake

Davy was eight, and for as long as he could remember he had lived with Granny at Granny's house. Davy loved Granny and Granny loved Davy, so it was a very good arrangement.

At the time of this story it was a cold January afternoon at the end of the school holidays. There didn't seem to be anything special about it; it was just an ordinary day. Davy had tomato soup for lunch. He bounced a tennis ball against the back of the house. He read his comic and coloured in a picture of a knight on a horse. For a minute or two he couldn't think what to do next.

Then he asked Granny if he could go and play in the park round the corner.

The only other person in the park

that day was the lady park-minder, but Davy didn't mind. He wanted to swing, which is something you can do perfectly well on your own. Davy took the swing up as high as he could. Higher and higher he swung, until he found he could see right behind the big bushes at the edge of the park.

He could see there was something lying on the ground there – something brightly coloured and curled up – but he couldn't quite see what it was, so he stopped the swing and went to find out.

It was a long, curled-up, tatty old

sausage-shaped thing, only it wasn't a thing.

It was a creature.

As Davy stood looking down at it, it blinked its eyes, sneezed and spoke.

'Darn leaves.'

It uncoiled itself and stretched out straight, craning its head up to look at him. It looked terribly thin, stretched out like that.

Davy crouched down so that it could see him better. 'My name's Davy. What's yours?'

'Snake,' replied the creature.

'Do you want to play?' Davy said.

'All right,' said Snake.

'Let's go to the pond,' suggested Davy.

So Davy walked and Snake slithered round the bushes. Davy thought the lady park-minder might have something to say about a great long snake slithering about in her park, but she just waved from her bench and carried on reading her book.

Davy looked down at his reflection in the pond. He dropped an old fir cone into it and watched the picture of himself shiver into nothing and put itself back together again.

'What's in there?' asked Snake. He peered over the edge of the pond and started back, his eyes wide with alarm. 'What's that?'

'That's you, Snake. Haven't you ever seen your reflection before?'

'What do you mean it's me? That's not me. This is me,' said Snake, puffing himself out. 'I don't think much of this game.' He gave an irritable sneeze and tucked his head under his tail.

'I'm sorry,' Davy said, crouching down again to give him a pat. 'Look, we'll do something else. Do you know how to make stones jump on the water?'

He looked doubtfully at Snake, who wasn't, after all, a very good shape for throwing things.

'Show me,' said Snake.

He slithered back to the water's edge and watched with interest as Davy selected a small flat stone and threw it so that it went skimming over the pond, bouncing three times before it sank.

'Not bad,' said Davy, choosing another stone. 'The best I've done is six.'

'Let me have a go,' said Snake. He

coiled himself into a single loop with his tail on top. 'Go on. Put it on my tail.'

So Davy did.

With a lightning flick of his tail Snake sent the stone flying out over the pond. One, two, three, four, five, six, seven times it skipped on the water before it sank.

Snake was cock-a-hoop. 'Did you see that? Did you see that? Seven! I bet there's not another darn snake alive who can –'

But just then, right in the middle of boasting, Snake began to sneeze and

sneeze and sneeze and sneeze and
sneeze. He sneezed so hard that Davy
was afraid he might sneeze himself
over the edge of the pond and fall in.

'Good grief,' Davy said. 'You'd
better get home to bed.'

'Aaatchoo!' sneezed Snake.

'Shall I take you home?' Davy asked.
'Do you live somewhere near?'

'Aaatchoo!' sneezed Snake.

Davy took off his scarf and wound it
round Snake from his head to his tail.
Snake was all damp and shivery.

'Could you put me back behind the
bushes?' he said. 'Aaatchoo!'

'But I can't leave you here,' Davy said.

'Just put me back, will you?'

He sounded so cantankerous that Davy carried him back without another word. Snake coiled up on the ground and shivered.

Davy squatted awkwardly beside him. 'I'll be seeing you, then,' he said.

Snake didn't reply. His eyes were closed.

'You can keep the scarf,' Davy said.

It was then that he had the most terrible thought. 'Snake, you do have a home to go to, don't you?' he asked.

Still Snake said nothing.

'You don't – you don't live here, do you?'

'Mind your own business,' wheezed Snake in a feeble voice. 'Aaatchoo!'

'But Snake, you can't. It's freezing cold and wet and horrible…'

Snake pretended to busy himself with his bed of leaves.

'Look,' said Davy. 'Why don't you come home with me?'

'Aaat-CHOO!' Snake sneezed his most enormous sneeze so far.

'Please,' Davy said.

Snake opened one feverish eye. 'All

right,' he said.

What happened next was that Davy carried Snake home, wheezing and sneezing, and Granny met them at the door.

'Granny, this is Snake,' Davy said.

Granny took one look at Snake, who could barely lift his head to say hello. 'My goodness,' Granny said. 'I've never seen such a woebegone, wet snake. You'd better bring him into the warm and dry him off. There's a fire in the sitting room. And I expect he'll be wanting some tea.' She hurried off into the kitchen.

Davy dried Snake with a towel, and set him down in an armchair by the fire, and tucked a big rug round him. He brought Snake hot buttered toast and ginger tea.

Snake felt sleepy after the ginger tea. 'You know I've got this bit of a cold?' he said between one yawn and the next. 'Will I stay here until it's gone?'

'This can be your home, Snake, if you want,' Davy said. 'I mean – well, you know – where you stay for good.'

A warm kind of ticklish feeling started inside Snake's tail and travelled all the way up to his head. He caught himself smiling and did his best to turn it into a cough.

'Darn crumbs,' said Snake. 'My home, did you say?'

And the smile came back, even bigger than before.

2

THE FIRST DAY OF SPRING

All through that first winter Snake got
fatter. The reason he got fatter was
that he was eating four big meals
every day – not to mention a number

of snake snacks in between.

In the end his skin began to split. It happened at breakfast, just as he was swallowing a mouthful of mashed banana. There was a loud tearing sound and Snake stopped in mid-swallow, not daring to move.

'Darn banana,' said Snake.

'Granny will put it right,' Davy said.

Granny was playing patience. Davy had to carry Snake up to her room because Snake didn't want to risk slithering.

Granny inspected him. 'Not to worry,' she said, and she opened her

sewing drawer. She pulled out a worn
pair of blue corduroy trousers, an old
green flannel nightshirt with stars on
it, and a faded brown velvet curtain.
She cut one good patch out of each
and sewed them carefully over Snake's
torn tummy. It prickled a bit but it
didn't really hurt.

'There you are,' she said, snipping
off the last piece of thread and giving
him a pat. 'Large as life and twice the
snake.'

'Thank you, Granny,' Davy said.

Out on the landing Snake examined
his patches. He thought they looked

fine, and he felt so sure of them that he slithered and bumped down the stairs all by himself.

'Let's go outside.'

'Okay,' Davy said, 'but you know the grass'll be wet. You ought to wear your coat.'

Snake grumbled all the time he was being buttoned up. Putting on a coat always seemed like such a darn long business.

He carried on grumbling until Davy opened the back door: then he stopped because he saw the garden. Something had happened there, and he couldn't remember ever seeing anything like it before. The sky was blue. The grass was soft and fine. There were little fuzzy buds on the tree, and underneath it was a whole crowd of white and purple flowers growing.

Snake looked up at Davy, who was good at answering questions.

'Crocuses,' said Davy.

Davy's boots made damp, soft prints on the grass. Snake's slithering made a soft damp squiggly trail.

The air was warm and fresh at once. It smelt of earth.

Davy said, 'It's the first day of spring.'

Snake didn't know what spring was, exactly, but he knew what it felt like. He gave a little squiggle, and another, and a wriggle, then he turned round and round in circles all because it was the first day of spring.

Just then Granny called down from the window to ask Davy if he'd mind helping her make a phone call. When she was on the phone Granny couldn't hear what the other person was saying. It was easier if someone else was there to listen and tell Granny what the person said.

'I'll be back in a minute,' said Davy
to Snake.

Now Snake had the first day of
spring all to himself. He made some
more squiggles. He lay still and
breathed in the smell of the grass. He
gazed up at the sky. He thought he
must be the most contented snake
alive.

It was spring. It was beautiful.

It was all too much.

Snake glided over to the crocuses
and before he knew what he was
doing he had bitten the heads off two

of them – snap snap – and another one – snap. He bit off a few more – snap snap snap. They tasted delicious.

Now he slithered right in among the crocuses and began to squiggle. At first he squiggled quite carefully, so only a few flowers got crushed, then he began to squiggle more wildly. He rolled on to his back to squiggle, and all the buttons on his coat dug into the earth and tore it up. At last he turned the right way up and found himself lying on a bed of mud, crushed grass, broken crocus heads and smashed stems.

For a moment or two Snake lay still,
with a heavy heart.

Then he slithered away and turned
back to survey the scene. It looked
terrible. He closed his eyes tight shut
and opened them again, but nothing
had changed. If anything it looked

even worse.

Snake went creeping behind the rain butt, where he was horribly sick. A cold draught made him shiver and the sky that had seemed so blue was suddenly grey and full of clouds. 'Poor Snake,' murmured Snake to himself. 'Poor, poor little Snake.'

He heard the back door open. He heard Davy's boots come squelching across the grass. He heard a long, awful silence. At last he heard Davy call his name, but he couldn't answer.

Snake decided he would stay behind the rain butt for ever. He would stay there until he died, and years later they would find his skin and gather it up and cry, and Davy would say –

But it wasn't going to happen like that, because all of a sudden Davy was there by the rain butt looking down at him. Snake lay still and tried to be invisible, but it wasn't any use. There he was, large as life and twice the snake, covered in earth, squashed petals and bits of grass.

'You did that?' Davy was so shocked that his voice was a whisper. 'You did all that by yourself?'

Snake lifted his head a fraction and

nodded miserably. There was no point in denying it.

Davy was so worried that Granny might discover what had happened that he didn't have room to be cross with Snake as well.

'We'd better get indoors quick and clean you up before Granny sees that coat.'

Snake hurried after Davy into the house, where they stuffed Snake's coat into the back of the washing machine. Davy dried the bits of earth on Snake's head with Granny's hairdryer and brushed them off with his hairbrush.

Davy and Snake were especially good and quiet until it got dark. Granny wouldn't go into the garden now, and even if she did she wouldn't be able to see what had happened. But what about tomorrow?

The next day was cold.

And the next was wet.

And the next was windy.

Each day that passed without Granny going out into the garden, or looking out and seeing what had happened, made Davy and Snake feel a bit easier. Snake kept watch while

Davy went to school, but Granny never opened the back door.

At the end of the week the weather turned warm again, but Granny had a cold and didn't go out.

On the tenth day Davy and Snake woke up very early. Davy looked at Snake and Snake looked at Davy.

'Let's go and look,' Davy said.

Snake shuddered at the thought, but he allowed Davy to button him into his coat.

Davy opened the back door. The air was sweet, the sky was blue – and Davy and Snake stopped still in their tracks.

Under the tree the grass was
growing, and there was a whole new
crowd of crocuses – yellow ones, now,
and even more of them than before.

'Is it the second first day of spring?'
asked Snake.

'I think it must be,' Davy said.

Snake squiggled for joy, though it
was a light little squiggle and it hardly
made a mark on the grass. He cast a
bright glance towards the crocuses,
growing so fresh and crisp under the
tree.

'They look nice, don't they, all those

darn croakies?' said Snake.

'Don't even think about it,' Davy
said.

3

Snake and the Most Important Thing

It was Sunday afternoon and Snake
was doing his exercises.

'One and two and loop to the left
and loop to the right and coil and

stretch… Darn it. That's wrong. It should have been stretch and coil.' He craned his head over to look at the page of diagrams in his instruction manual and prepared to start again.

Davy groaned. 'Do you have to go all the way back to the beginning every time you make a mistake?'

'Of course I do,' said Snake. 'How else am I supposed to know where I am?'

'Well I wish you'd get a move on,' said Davy. 'I don't want to spend the whole day watching you coil when you're meant to be stretching.'

The last exercise in Snake's book, when he finally reached it, required him to hang upside-down from the banisters. Almost as soon as he'd got himself into position he cried out, 'I'm slipping, I'm slipping,' and Davy had to rescue him fast. By now he was in a poor state, gasping for mango juice.

Delivered by Davy in a tall glass, and siphoned up through a straw by Snake, the mango juice had an almost magical effect. Snake slithered off down the stairs to tackle the next stage of his training: three laps round the garden. Davy's job was to record his time.

Snake finished the first lap in style. 'Six minutes thirty seconds,' Davy announced. The second lap took longer. 'Eight minutes fourteen seconds,' said Davy. 'Maybe you could give the third lap a miss just this once?'

But Snake wouldn't hear of it. He crept on, ever more slowly, round the edge of the garden, until at last he reached the back door and lay stretched out in a line. He had a bad stitch.

'Fifteen minutes fifty-three

seconds,' said Davy. 'And it's time for lunch.'

Snake had set his heart on an athletic career after watching a television programme which followed the progress of a group of children in training. He had considered various possibilities, including the high jump, hurdling and javelin-throwing, before settling for the idea of being the fastest slitherer in the world.

Over lunch, in between mouthfuls of spinach, he stretched out his neck, arched his back and flexed the tip of his tail, just to show he was an athlete in the making. 'The most important thing', he bragged with his mouth full, 'is to be in peak condition. If you're in peak condition you can do whatever you like.'

Davy had promised to give Snake a swimming lesson as soon as his lunch had gone down, and Snake was greatly looking forward to it.

He draped himself over the back of the bath and Davy held on to his tail. The idea was that when Davy let go Snake should slide down head-first into the water, which he successfully did. He then thrashed about briefly before sinking like a stone to the bottom.

Davy hauled him out and offered to find him something to help him float, but Snake had had enough. With a very bad grace, dripping and cursing, he allowed Davy to wring him out and dry him off. 'Darn training facilities in this house are useless,' he complained. 'I'm never going to get into peak condition at this rate.'

Davy left him bundled up in a towel so that only his two glowering eyes were showing and hurried downstairs to make toasted cheese.

After tea Davy and Snake lay on the sitting-room floor and played cards. Snake was so tired he could hardly keep his eyes open, let alone say 'Snap,' and had to be carried up to bed.

'Never mind, Snake,' said Davy, tucking him in. 'Perhaps it'll be easier tomorrow.'

Snake didn't reply. He was already asleep.

The morning was half over before Snake came slithering heavily down the stairs, bleary-eyed and moaning.

'Honestly, Snake. Anyone would

think you'd run a marathon,' said Davy.

'I feel as if I've run a marathon,' said Snake bitterly. 'I can hardly move and I hurt all over and I'm probably getting a cold from that darn horrible swimming.' He huddled over his porridge and shivered.

'Well if you're serious about getting into peak condition you'd better hurry up and get started on your exercises,' Davy said.

Snake gave him a look of dislike and ate his breakfast very slowly.

Eventually, when he couldn't put it

off any longer, he trailed back up to the landing. He looped to the left and looped to the right and coiled and stretched and stretched and coiled, but his heart just wasn't in it.

'Come on, Snake,' said Davy. 'You won't get anywhere like that.'

Snake's reply was not polite.

The moment arrived – none too soon, in Snake's opinion – for the final hanging-upside-down exercise. Davy fastened his tail to the banister and Snake swung out into the hallway. He hung there, swaying gently back and forth.

It was very peaceful upside-down.

Nothing happened for a while,
except that Granny moved from the
kitchen to the sitting room with a cup
of coffee and a newspaper. She didn't
look up so she didn't even know
Snake was there. But everything
looked different
and interesting upside-down.

Snake began to wonder: what floor
was he on, hanging down like this? He
wasn't on the top floor, for sure, but
he wasn't on the ground floor either.
He was on both, and at the same time
he wasn't on either. Perhaps that

meant he wasn't anywhere at all.

Snake began to feel dizzy. He cried out: 'Davy!'

Davy came quickly to pull him up. 'Were you slipping again?'

'I just had a thought,' said Snake.

'What was that?' Davy asked.

'This peak condi-tion business,' said Snake. 'It's all very

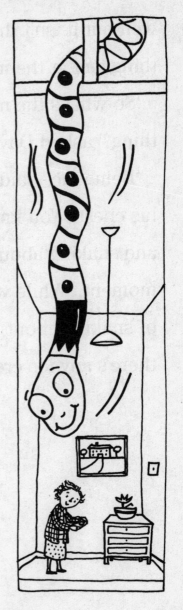

well but it isn't the most important thing just at the minute.'

'So what's the most important thing?' asked Davy.

'Being me,' said Snake, puffing out his chest. 'You know. Just being me and snaking about.' He fell silent for a moment. 'While we're on the subject of snaking about, do you suppose there's any ice cream in the fridge?'

4

A PRESENT FOR GRANNY

Davy and Snake were holding an
emergency meeting. Anyone who
could have seen their faces would
have thought they were in trouble, and

they were. The trouble was that it was Saturday, and Granny's birthday was on Monday. 'That means we've got two days,' said Davy gloomily. 'Two days counting today, and no present for Granny.' He sorted through the coins in his money box and shook his head. 'Nineteen pence.'

'I've got some, don't forget,' said Snake. Davy waited out of politeness but he already knew exactly how much money Snake had because Snake counted it every night before he went to sleep. Snake had a five pence piece that he'd found down the back of the armchair in the bathroom and two pence that the postman, who was a friend of Snake's, had given him. Snake kept his money in an old sock and now he burrowed into the toe to investigate its contents. 'One big one – that's two pence – and one little one – that's five. Seven altogether,' he announced.

'Exactly,' said Davy. 'We have twenty-six pence between us. That's hardly enough to buy anything.'

'Isn't twenty-six pence very many?' asked Snake.

'Not very many at all,' Davy said.

'Darn it,' said Snake.

There was a mournful silence while Davy and Snake contemplated the situation.

'Do you think she'd like a button?' asked Snake brightly. 'There's a nice one under your bed.

'It's a big one with four holes,' he went on, less brightly now. Davy's face was bleak.

'She could sew it on something. Or keep it as a spare.' Snake's voice wavered, on the brink of tears. He hated it when Davy didn't know what to do. It made everything seem all wrong and out of sorts.

Davy sighed. He saw that on top of the problem of Granny's present he now had another problem on his hands: a snake who needed cheering up in a hurry. 'Come on, then. Let's go and look at it.'

The button Snake retrieved from under Davy's bed and laid at his feet was silvery-smooth, like the inside of a shell. It glowed in the sun.

Davy hadn't expected anything of it, but now that he had seen it he began to have an idea. 'Snake, you're brilliant.'

Festooned with eyebrows of fluff from under the bed, Snake tried to look modest and failed.

Davy whisked an empty shoebox off the bedside table. He had always thought it would come in useful and now he knew exactly what to do with it. 'We can make a treasure box for Granny. Don't you think that would be a good birthday present?'

'What about my button then?' asked Snake. His voice was dim with disappointment.

'Your button is the first piece of treasure, you dope. It was your button that gave me the idea.'

Snake puffed himself out, fat with self-importance. 'Of course,' he said. 'Open the darn box then,' and he dropped the button in.

'We'll have to keep the box under the bed so Granny won't see it,' Davy said. 'Now all we need is more treasures to put in it.'

'We could put in an egg,' suggested Snake.

'It might break,' Davy objected.

'A hard-boiled egg then,' said Snake. 'And I'll paint it.'

'I'll put in my twig pencil,' said Davy.

'Granny likes drawing.'

'We could find a nice stone,' said Snake.

'She could use it as a paperweight,' said Davy.

'I might put in my toothbrush,' said Snake, who had never been keen on having his teeth brushed.

'I don't think Granny would want your toothbrush, Snake,' said Davy.

'What's wrong with my toothbrush?' said Snake.

By Saturday evening there were lots of things in the treasure box: the silvery-smooth button, a hard-boiled egg decorated by Snake with splodges of red and green, a flat grey speckled stone from the park, the twig pencil, a wren feather, a ball of sparkly thread that Davy had bought in the winter to tie up his Christmas presents with, and a crossword cut out of the newspaper. Davy and Snake slept extremely well.

On Sunday they added a tangerine left over from lunch and a packet of poppy seeds that had slipped down behind the jars on the kitchen shelf. Davy put in a tiny book he had made at school, full of stick men having adventures. Snake put in a Russian postage stamp from under the stair carpet and a little black key he had found in the garden. Last of all they put in a packet of raisins, bought for twenty-five pence from the shop on the corner and a single penny piece, polished by Davy until it shone.

They painted the sides of the box with coloured snakes and stars. Davy was the one to write 'Happy Birthday, Granny' on the lid because he was better at spelling than Snake, but Snake got to paint all round it.

On Monday morning they were up at seven, waiting in the kitchen for Granny to come down to breakfast.

'My word,' she said when she saw the treasure box, lying in her place on the breakfast table. 'What's this?'

'It's a treasure box,' said Davy.

'For you,' said Snake.

'For your birthday,' Davy said.

'Happy birthday,' cried Snake.

Granny opened the box and took out her presents one by one. The first thing she took out was the shell button. 'What a beautiful button!' she said. 'It's just what I need to fasten the collar on my gardening coat. And I've been looking for a stone like this for ages. Now I'll be able to keep all my papers from blowing away. And my goodness me, I thought I'd lost this for ever!'

It was the little black key.

'I found it,' said Snake, puffed out and squiggling with excitement at the success of the treasure box. 'In the flowerbed by the compost heap.'

'Then you're a very, very clever Snake,' Granny said. 'I always thought you were.'

'What is it the key to, Granny?' asked Davy.

'Well,' Granny replied. 'I won't tell you now, but I'll tell you in six months' time.'

Snake couldn't imagine six months but Davy counted them on his fingers. 'December? Why can't you tell us now?'

'You'll see,' Granny said. 'In the mean time, I'm so pleased with my birthday presents. Can I put the egg up here on the shelf where I can see it every day? And the little book? I think I'll put the feather in a jar.'

Davy liked mysteries. He tucked away the mystery of the little key and turned his attention back to Granny's presents. 'I put in the pencil,' he said.

'I put in the button,' said Snake. 'And the stamp.'

'I found the poppy seeds,' said Davy.

'But the button was first,' said Snake.

And they all settled down to an
extra-special birthday breakfast.

And they all settled down to an
extra-special early breakfast.

5

THE FAMILY TREE

Davy was doing his homework. Snake
was pretending to read a book and
trying to put Davy off.

Snake threw back his head and
chortled, as if he'd just read

something very funny. He thought
Davy might at least ask what it was,
but Davy was so engrossed in what he
was doing that he didn't even look up.

Snake heaved a heavy sigh as if he
had a bad worry on his mind. Davy
didn't seem to notice that either.

Finally Snake started coughing,
which was difficult at first, since he
didn't really have a tickle, but got
easier as he went along. At last Davy
looked up and banged him on the
back. 'I'll get you some ginger tea.'

Davy went to put the kettle on, and
Snake took a look at the homework.

All Davy seemed to have done was to make a list of names on one piece of paper and draw a few straight lines on another. Most of the lines didn't even join up.

Davy came back with the tea. Snake gave a little cough, for form's sake, and looked forward to a good chat. But Davy simply passed Snake his cup, set down his own, and began once again to stare dreamily at the page with the lines on it. Snake found it very annoying.

'What is that thing?' said Snake, drawing vengefully on his tea.

'It's a family tree,' said Davy. 'You write the names in these spaces, and they tell you who all the members of your family are. You know, who married who and who had who.'

Very carefully, in his best handwriting, he filled in the names:

Snake looked at the family tree. It

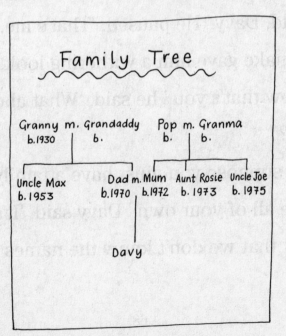

```
                Family Tree
               ~~~~~~~~~~~~

   Granny m. Grandaddy    Pop m. Granma
   b.1930    b.            b.    b.

   |_____|            |_____|
   |           |            |          |          |
 Uncle Max   Dad m. Mum   Aunt Rosie  Uncle Joe
 b.1953    b.1970  b.1972  b.1973      b.1975

              |
             Davy
```

didn't seem to make a lot more sense than it had before. Davy did his best to explain it. 'Granny married Grandaddy and they had two children, Uncle Max and Dad. Pop married Granma and they had three children, Mum, Aunt Rosie and Uncle Joe. Then Dad married Mum and they had one child, Davy.' He paused. 'That's me.'

Snake gave him a withering look. 'I know that's you,' he said. 'What about me?'

'I suppose you must have a family tree all of your own,' Davy said. 'It's just that we don't know the names of all the snakes on it. Your mother and father wouldn't have got married exactly…' He trailed off doubtfully, catching sight of Snake's face. 'And you wouldn't put "*b*" for "born". I guess you'd have to put "*h*" for hatched.'

Snake was outraged. 'Hatched? Hatched? What would you want to put that for?'

'Snakes hatch – ' faltered Davy '– out of eggs. You would have hatched–'

'I did not hatch out of an egg,' interrupted Snake. 'And if all you can do is insult me I shall go elsewhere.'

Snake retreated to a corner of the room, where he maintained a huffy silence for the rest of the evening. He refused the offer of a second cup of ginger tea, and also of supper. This dignity demanded, even though supper was macaroni cheese with tomato salad, which happened to be one of his favourites. Several times Davy tried to start a conversation, but Snake wouldn't have it. When Davy said that he was going up to bed, Snake announced that he would sleep in the sitting room, and nothing Davy could say would persuade him otherwise.

As soon as Davy had gone upstairs, Snake came back to the table and tugged the family tree out of Davy's homework folder.

He rooted about in Davy's pencil case for a red felt pen.

In the space next to Davy's name he wrote SNAKE in big red capital letters and underlined it three times.

He drew one thick line connecting SNAKE to Davy and another connecting SNAKE to Granny. He decorated the whole page with exclamation marks and added a zigzag border. If you asked Snake, the family tree looked a lot more interesting than it had before.

Snake slipped it back into the folder and slithered off to an armchair to sleep. He made a good nest of cushions, but however much he squiggled and wriggled and tossed and turned he couldn't get off to sleep. At half past midnight he fetched Davy's old school jersey from the table, coiled himself up inside it and slept at last.

Snake dreamt that Davy's teacher was looking at Davy's decorated family tree and demanding to know who was responsible for it. 'This snake is a genius,' she said. 'There's no other word for it.'

Snake was just moving on to another highly satisfactory scene in this dream, in which his works were being exhibited to universal acclaim, when Davy came into the room with toast and honey and a cup of tea. He drew the curtains.

'I've brought your breakfast,' said Davy, putting it down beside him.

Snake struggled out of one of the sleeves of the jersey. He was still feeling scratchy. Without looking at

THE EDUCATION COMMITTEE
ST ANDREW'S HIGH SCHOOL
KIRKCALDY

Davy he took little snaps at the toast.

'Friends?' Davy asked.

'If you want,' said Snake in his most
unfriendly voice.

Davy went over to the table to pick
up his homework. Snake swallowed
hard. For some reason he felt nervous

Friends?

all of a sudden.

'Um. That darn tree of yours,' said Snake. 'Do you have to hand it in today?'

'Tomorrow,' said Davy. 'I just have to ask Granny for some dates so that I can finish it off tonight. It's looking pretty good. Do you want to see?'

Before Snake could say anything, Davy had taken the family tree out of the folder. Snake could see the red marks he'd made coming right through the paper. He burrowed his way back into the jersey and lay very still, waiting for the storm to break.

When Davy spoke his voice was very quiet and calm.

'You've wrecked it,' said Davy. 'You've wrecked my family tree. How could you do that?'

Snake darted his head out of the jersey for as long as it took him to shout, 'You left me out!' Two seconds later he emerged again to shout, 'I don't want to be on your darn tree anyway!'

And at that moment Granny came in. 'Davy? I'm going to plant that little beech. Do you want to come and help? You've got time if we do it straight away.'

Davy followed her to the door. Snake watched them with one murderous eye through a hole in the jersey. At the last minute Davy came back and picked him up. 'I'll bring Snake. He could do with some fresh air.'

Granny and Davy and Snake went out into the garden. Granny dug a hole and Davy put the beech plant in it. He patted down the soil all round and Granny watered it.

Snake lay on the grass and wished he was close enough to bite Davy's leg.

But before he could do anything about it Davy had picked him up and they were all three together, looking down at the new tree. Davy gave Snake a squeeze just where the toast and honey had got to, which felt nice and not nice both at once.

'Doesn't that look fine?' said Granny. 'I don't think we could ask for a better little tree.'

'We couldn't,' Davy said. 'It's our own real family tree.'